Hubley, Penny
 Italian Family. – (Beans. Geography)
 1. Family – Italy
 I. Title
 306.8'5'0945   HQ630
 ISBN 0–7136–2731–X

A & C Black (Publishers) Limited
35 Bedford Row, London WC1R 4JH

© 1986 text and photographs Penny and John Hubley

Acknowledgements
The map is by Tony Garrett

Filmset by August Filmsetting, Haydock, St. Helens
Printed in Hong Kong by Dai Nippon Printing Co. Ltd

Italian Family

Penny and John Hubley

A & C Black · London

Milan

Parm

Genoa

LIGURIAN

SEA

This is Francesca Rossi.
She's eight years old
and lives in Grassina in
Northern Italy.
Grassina is a small town
about ten kilometres
from Florence. It's a
very old town and its
name comes from a
Roman family who once
lived there.

GERMANY   AUSTRIA

SWITZ-
ERLAND

FRANCE

I
T
A
L
Y

Florence

Rome

Y U G O S L A V I A

Pisa

Sardinia

Mediterranean Sea

Sicily

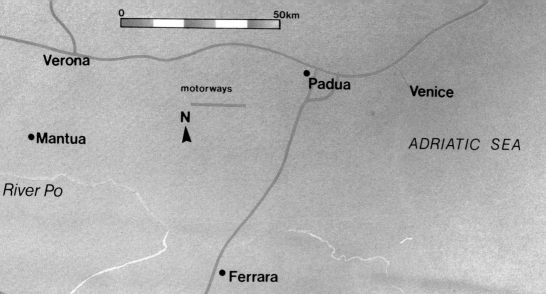

Francesca has lived in Grassina for only three years. Before that her family lived in the country, near a town called Greve. They decided to move so that Francesca's dad could be nearer to his work. Francesca's grandparents still live in Greve, and she often goes to see them. It only takes thirty minutes by car but it's a twisty mountain road and it seems like a long journey.

3

Francesca and her parents live in a new block of flats, on the first floor. Francesca likes the flat because it was built specially for her family.

When the family decided to move to Grassina, they joined up with a group of people called a co-operative. Some people in the co-operative were friends and some had seen it advertised in newspapers. The group all worked together to build the flats. They borrowed money from a bank, and hired the architects and builders. When the flats were built, everyone moved in.

Behind the flats there's a big garden that everybody shares. The garden was the last thing to be finished. Francesca's family and their neighbours had a huge party to celebrate and everyone brought food. Francesca's dad brought some ham and carved a piece for everyone.

They wanted to have the party in the garden, but when the day came it poured with rain, so they had to hold the party under cover by the car park. It was such a good party that nobody minded.

Every morning at eight o'clock Francesca catches the school bus with her friends. Her school is on the other side of town. It's called the Scuola Elementaria Marconi, named after a famous Italian inventor.

On weekdays Francesca is at school from half past eight until half past four. There's school on Saturday mornings too. Most primary schools have shorter hours but Francesca's mum and dad send her to this one because they have to work all day.

Francesca's in the second grade with twenty five other children in her class. She's best at writing stories and drawing pictures. She doesn't like P.E. at all.

Because the day is so long, the class has two different teachers. There's one for the mornings and another for the afternoons. Nearly everybody in the class likes the morning teacher because she often brings her guitar and they all join in singing. There's one song that Francesca likes best. It's hard to sing, though, because the words are in French and Russian and English as well as Italian.

Francesca stays at school for lunch. There isn't a school dining room so they clear all the books away and eat at their desks. The food is cooked in the school kitchens and everybody takes it in turns to serve. Today they're having chicken which is Francesca's favourite.

During the day there are long breaks when
everyone goes out into the school playground. The
boys all play football which is called 'calcio' in
Italy. Grassina has two amateur clubs but most of
the boys support Fiorentina which is Florence's
professional team.

Francesca's dad used to play football when he was
a boy. Now he's a keen volleyball fan. He supports
the Grassina team and sometimes takes Francesca
to the league games. Home matches are played at
the Casa di Populo. This is the working men's club
which is used as the town community centre. The
Grassina team won the national championship
there this year.

At the end of June, school breaks up for three months. During the holiday, Francesca sometimes takes the bus to Florence for the day to visit her cousins. Before the bus arrives she has to buy tickets from a coffee bar.

In Florence there are always thousands of tourists. They fill all the bars and street cafes. Most of them come to see the famous buildings and paintings. The city gets so crowded in the summer that the tourists stay in hotels as far away as Grassina.

Florence is a very old city. It was founded by soldiers from Julius Caesar's army who called it Florentia. Its modern name in Italian is Firenze. Near Florence you can see buildings that the Romans left. The small picture shows one of their theatres. In the past, Florence and the other cities of Italy each had their own rulers. Italy became one nation in the last century and for five years Florence was the capital city. Rome became the capital in 1870.

Francesca's family go away from Grassina on holiday for the first two weeks of August. This is a national holiday in Italy and all the factories and shops close down. It's called Feragosto which means August Fair. Most years the Rossis have a holiday at the seaside on the west coast of Italy.

Francesca's dad, Alberto, works in a factory in the north of Florence. There aren't any large factories in Grassina so a lot of people travel to work in the city. Signor Rossi drives there every day in his new car. It's an Italian Fiat and he's very proud of it. Every weekend he spends time polishing it and tinkering with the engine.

Signor Rossi's job is to make moulds for plastic bottles. He makes the moulds from strong metal and then neatens any rough edges using special drills. It is a very skilled job and it took him years to learn.

When the moulds are ready they are sent to other factories where the bottles are made. Hot plastic is blown into a mould. As the plastic cools off it hardens into a bottle shape. The mould is taken off and the bottle is finished. Here are some of the bottles labelled and filled.

The factory where Francesca's dad works is small, but the moulds that he makes are sent to places all over the world including Britain, North America and the Middle East.

Francesca's mum, Renata, works at home as a dressmaker. A company delivers the cloth to the flats. It's all cut out and ready to sew. Signora Rossi and her neighbours divide the work between them. At the moment she is sewing the company's label into a ladies' blouse.

Because she likes fresh food, Signora Rossi goes shopping nearly every day. She can get everything she needs from the shops in Grassina.

The first thing on her shopping list is a joint of lamb which she gets from the butcher's. Then on to the fishmonger's van to buy some clams. She'll cook them in a sauce to eat with spaghetti.

Next Signora Rossi gets half a kilo of the local farmhouse cheese and stocks up on ham. On Fridays there's an open air market in the town square. Signora Rossi buys her fruit and vegetables from a stall there because they're usually fresh each day.

Francesca's dad loves salami so her mum picks out a couple of good ones. She mustn't forget to buy a magazine for Francesca. It tells you what's on TV each week, and with nine channels to choose from, that's really useful.

The last thing on Signora Rossi's list is pasta. The family start their evening meal with pasta, usually with tomato sauce on top. Then they have meat and vegetables, and fresh fruit to follow.

Francesca's mum usually buys dried pasta from the supermarket. It isn't as nice as fresh pasta but it's much cheaper. She only gets fresh pasta for special occasions.

Signor Rossi has a friend who runs a small business making pasta. The pasta comes in all sorts of shapes and sizes. The most popular kind is spaghetti. The machine in the picture is making tortellini. These are little pasta pockets stuffed with a meat filling.

Pasta is made from wheat mixed with oil, water and salt. The dough is flattened into a huge sheet. Then the machine cuts out pieces of dough and wraps them round a little bit of filling. A fan blows air onto the pasta to stop it from sticking to the machine.

On her way home Francesca's mum stops for a coffee at the Bar Sergio. She usually drinks her coffee standing inside at the bar. In summer people can sit at the tables on the pavement outside. Signora Rossi doesn't often do this because if you sit down, you have to pay more.

You can buy all sorts of fresh cakes, pastries and biscuits at the bar. The pastry cook is an old friend of the Rossi family, called Mario. He has to start work at four o'clock in the morning so that the pastries are ready when the bar opens three hours later.

Francesca's favourite biscuits are the ones with jam on top. When she goes there with her mum, Mario always slips an extra biscuit into the bag as a treat.

The bar is open every day except Tuesdays, and doesn't shut until nine in the evening. People use it as a meeting place to stop and chat. There are eight bars in Grassina, and each one has its regular customers who go to have coffee and a snack before work.

At weekends Francesca's mum and dad often take her to visit her grandparents. They live in an old farmhouse in Greve, which is about nineteen kilometres from Grassina.

Francesca loves going for walks with her grandad. She thinks it would be rather nice to live in the country but her dad says that it's hard work living on a farm.

Her grandfather grows peaches, apricots, olives and grapes. Most of these are traded with neighbours for other goods such as meat and cheese, or for the loan of farm equipment. Anything that's left over is sold in the local market.

Grandad's pride is his kitchen garden. In it he grows vegetables for the family. He's especially proud of his artichokes, tomatoes and lettuces, and waters them carefully through the long dry summer.

Spring is a busy time for Francesca's grandad. If he doesn't cut back the olive trees, they grow spindly and don't produce many olives. Although he is quite an old man, he climbs the ladder to prune them himself. He says that some of the trees are a hundred years old and still producing olives.

Francesca's grandad doesn't keep animals any more because he finds it difficult to manage the farm on his own. He understands why his sons took jobs in the city but he's sad that there is no one else to take over the farm.

23

On the farm Francesca's grandfather grows grapes. He makes his own wine for the family to drink with their meals. The farm is in the Chianti region of Italy which is famous for red wine.

Nearby there is an ancient castle which once belonged to an early explorer of America, called Giovanni da Verrazzano. A statue of him stands in the Greve market square. His family still live in the castle and make wine.

It's spring now so the grapevines are cut back and tied to supports with willow twigs to make sure that they grow up straight.

The grapes start to grow in the summer and by October they are ripe and ready to be picked. The juice is squeezed out in a huge press. Then it is kept in large oak barrels to ferment into wine.

When the wine is ready to drink it is put into bottles. On the labels there is a picture of Giovanni da Verrazzano. Most of the wine is sent out to the USA, and to other countries in Europe, but some even goes to Australia.

Francesca's grandparents are busy in the spring but they always find time to invite the whole family round for Easter dinner. Francesca tells them how excited she is about the raffle tickets she has bought. Every bar has an Easter raffle and Francesca thinks she might be lucky and win a giant chocolate egg.

Although many people in Italy are devout Catholics, the Rossi family don't go to church. They do join in some of the Easter celebrations, and everyone helps to prepare dinner on Easter Sunday.

Grandad opens a bottle of his home-made wine,
Mum cooks the pasta and Dad does the chicken.
Then they end their meal with a special traditional
cross-shaped cake.